ESTEMMENOSUCHUS

AGUSTINIA

MAJUNGASAURUS

ALAMOSAURUS

CEARADACTYLUS

GIGANOTOSAURUS

KOSMOCERATOPS

CONCAVENATOR

HYPACROSAURUS

ENIGMOSAURUS

JANE YOLEN

How Do Dinosaurs

Stay Safe?

Illustrated by

MARK TEAGUE

THE BLUE SKY PRESS
An Imprint of Scholastic Inc. · New York

HOW DO PARENTS AND TEACHERS TALK ABOUT SAFETY?

It's normal for children to explore the world and test their limits.
But sometimes, even with the best of intentions, curiosity can
lead to behavior that can cause problems. The humorous antics
of the dinosaurs in this book are both a source of entertainment
and—we hope—an opportunity for parents and teachers to discuss
additional safety issues. Maybe this book can be some small help
as your little dinosaurs learn how to stay safe and play safe.

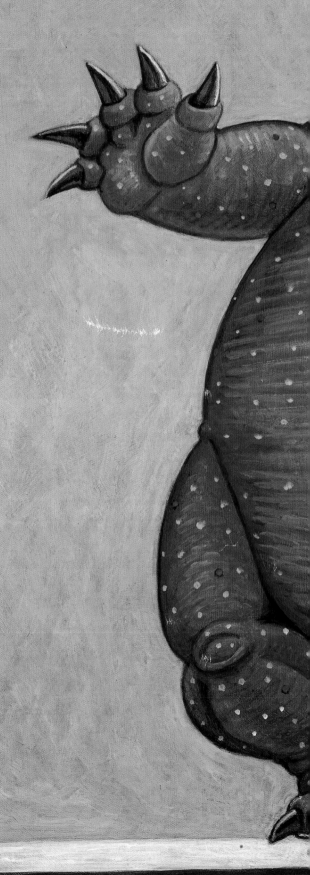

THE BLUE SKY PRESS

Text copyright © 2015 by Jane Yolen

Illustrations copyright © 2015 by Mark Teague

Library of Congress card catalog number: 2014012577

ISBN 978-0-439-24104-5

10 9 8 7 6 5 4   17 18 19

Printed in Malaysia   108

First printing, March 2015

Designed by Kathleen Westray

For Juliet Grenzke:
longed for, waited for,
here at last . . .
—Nana Jane

For Tsarmina
—M. T.

How does
a dinosaur
stay safe
all day?
Whether
at home or
at school
or at play?

Does he

climb up

too high?

ALAMOSAURUS

Does he race on his bike
with no helmet
on head?

Is he rough with the cat?
Does he stand up
on chairs?

KOSMOCERATOPS

HYPACROSAURUS

When Mama says "No!"
does he run down the stairs?

If anyone dares him,
does he always try

to jump from the rooftop
as if he could fly?

No . . .

a dinosaur doesn't—

and I'll tell you why.

When crossing the street,
he holds Mama's
hand tight.
And he's ever so watchful
to cross with
the light.

He's careful with forks,
knives, and spoons
when he eats.

He never goes off
with the strangers
he meets.

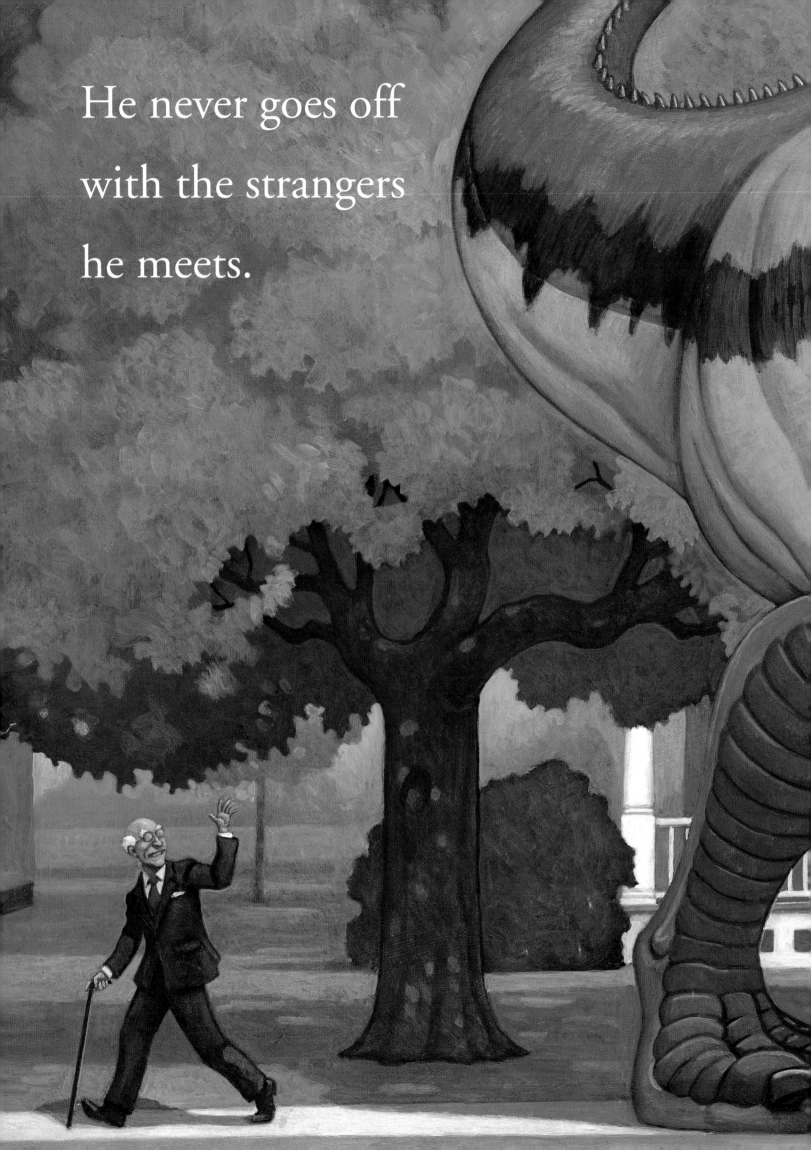

When swimming with friends

he is careful to be

right at the spot

where his papa can see.

He wears
a good helmet
when riding a bike,

CONCAVENATOR

takes bottles of water

when on a long hike.

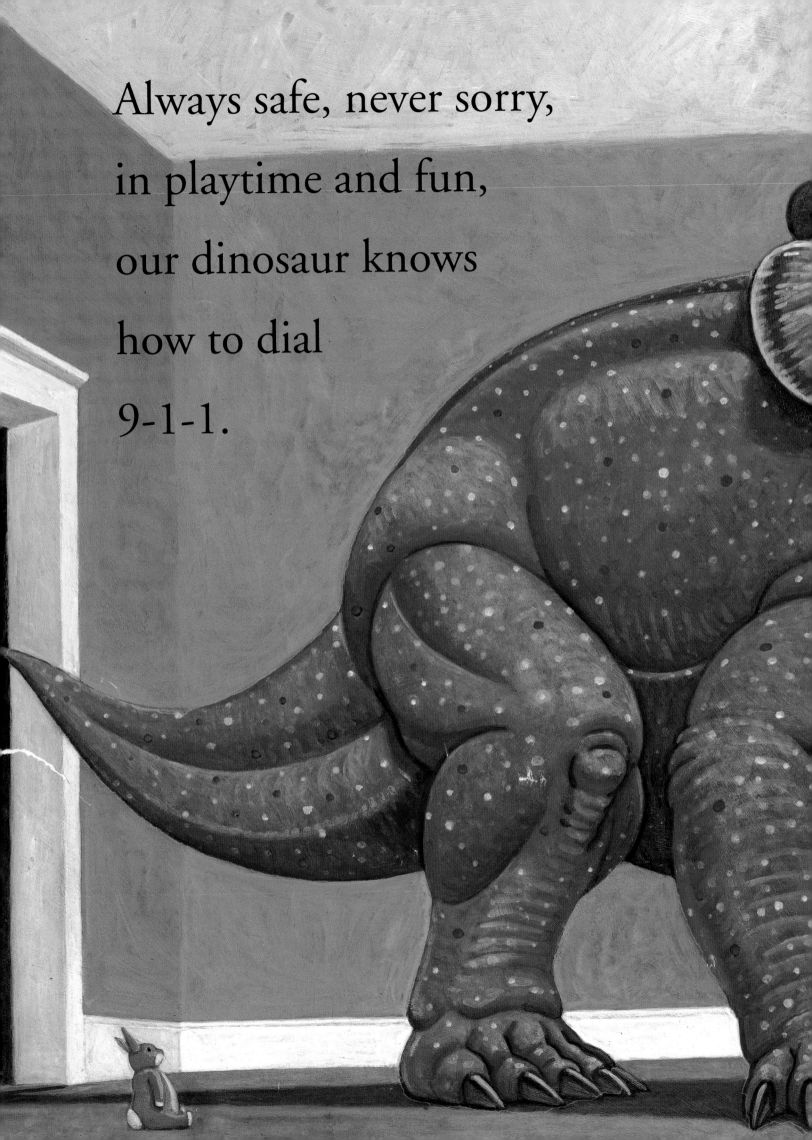

Always safe, never sorry,
in playtime and fun,
our dinosaur knows
how to dial
9-1-1.

He's careful—
not fearful.
So here's a
big roar.

Stay safe, and PLAY safe,

little dinosaur.

ESTEMMENOSUCHUS

AGUSTINIA

MAJUNGASAURUS

ALAMOSAURUS

CEARADACTYLUS

GIGANOTOSAURUS

KOSMOCERATOPS

CONCAVENATOR

HYPACROSAURUS

ENIGMOSAURUS